D.W. FLIPS!

Marc Brown

LITTLE, BROWN AND COMPANY

New York ⌁ Boston

with love for
Eliza Morgan Brown

Little, Brown and Company
Hachette Book Group USA
237 Park Avenue, New York, NY 10017
Visit our Web site at www.lb-kids.com

D.W.® is a registered trademark of Marc Brown.

First Paperback Edition: April 1991

ISBN 978-0-316-11269-7

Library of Congress Catalog Card Number 86-27640
Library of Congress Cataloging-in-Publication information is available.

10   9   8

Published simultaneously in Canada by Little, Brown & Company (Canada) Limited

Manufactured in China

SC

"I can't believe they put me in this baby class," said D.W. "I want to do flips."

Miss Morgan put on music.
"First we do warm-ups," she said.
"Up, down, touch your toes.
Very good."

"Everyone join hands and skip in a circle.
Slow. Now faster," said Miss Morgan.

"Not that fast!" she said.
She blew her whistle.
"Now we will learn the forward roll.
Watch carefully," said Miss Morgan.

"Bend your knees,

hands down,

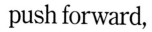
tuck your head under,

push forward,

over and up!"

"Everyone try it," said Miss Morgan.
"This will be easy," said D.W.
"Who wants to be first?" asked Miss Morgan.
"I do!" said Emily.

"Very good, Emily," said Miss Morgan.
"D.W., you're next."

Whump!
"Don't worry, D.W.," said Miss Morgan.
"You will learn. It takes time."
"Lots of time," said Emily.

Everyone practiced forward rolls.
"Need some help?" asked Emily.
"That's all for today," said Miss Morgan.
"Don't forget to practice!"

D.W. practiced in her room every night.

She practiced in the dining room.

She practiced in the laundry room.

She practiced everywhere.

Finally it was time for D.W.'s next class.

"Who remembers what we did last week?"
asked Miss Morgan.
D.W. jumped up.
"Everyone watch D.W.," said Miss
Morgan.
"Are you sure you're ready?" said
Emily.

D.W. rolled forward once,

twice,

three times.

"Wow!" said Emily.
"Good work," said Miss Morgan.
"Thanks," said D.W.

"Now," said Miss Morgan,
"we will try something new—

backward rolls."